SLEEPING NANNA

KEVIN CROSSLEY-HOLLAND

PICTURES BY
PETER MELNYCZUK

ORCHARD
BOOKS
LONDON

For Gillian and Oenone
Kevin Crossley-Holland

For my family
Peter Melnyczuk

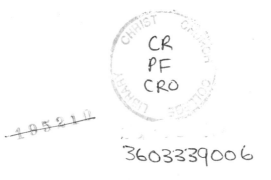
Text copyright © Kevin Crossley-Holland 1989
Illustrations copyright © Peter Melnyczuk 1989
First published in Great Britain in 1989 by
ORCHARD BOOKS
96 Leonard Street, London EC2A 4RH
Orchard Books Australia
14 Mars Road, Lane Cove, NSW 2066
1 85213 048 2
Printed and bound in
Belgium

"I can't," said Nanna.

"You will," said her mother. "Sleep well, Nanna."

"Can't," repeated Nanna.

"Cuckoo!" sang the bright-eye in the dusty clock.

"Whoomph!" barged the wind.

"Pitterpitterpitter," pattered the attic mice . . .

When Nanna opened her eyes, a boy was standing at the end of the bed.

"You can come with me if you like," said the boy.

"Where are you going?" asked Nanna.

"To my own kingdom," said the boy. "My boat's by the bridge."

Nanna jumped out of bed and put on her dressing-gown and slippers. Then they ran down to the stream where the boy's boat was waiting.

Nanna sat down in the stern and heard the water swilling and sucking and gurgling under her feet.

"Where is your kingdom?" Nanna asked.

"Over the sea," said the boy. "Down the stream and into the river and over the sea."

The little boat began to glide downstream. It went faster than Nanna's questions; they got left behind, bubbles floating on the dark face of the stream.

As the river opened its arms to the sea, the boy hoisted a little sail, and a blue flag with a white square in the middle—a fluttering Blue Peter.

"Where now?" asked Nanna.

"East over the breakers," the boy said. And away they danced over the singing silver-and-navy sea.

"That's my kingdom," said the boy, pointing.

"A little island!" cried Nanna. "A blue island!"

"That's its name," said the boy. "Blue Island! Everything you can see is blue. Blue cheese, blue stockings, bluebottles . . . And once in a blue moon, I've even seen the Blue Bird of Happiness."

"Oh!" cried Nanna.

"Look!" said the boy. "There's every kind of blue: cobalt, azure, prussian, lapis . . ."

"I don't know those names," Nanna exclaimed. "Will you show me?"

The boy shook his head. "This is where you must leave me," he said. "You must sail on under this Blue Peter."

"Alone?" asked Nanna.

"Alone," said the boy.

As the boat scraped the shingle the boy jumped out
of the boat and picked up a blue stone, shaped like an egg.
"Take this!" said the boy. "My boat will bring you
to four more islands, and then we'll meet again."
The boy pushed the boat back into deep waters
and Nanna waved. Then she looked at her stone and
saw that it was the colour of dawn and sad songs and
gentians: blue of blue.

It wasn't long before Nanna sighted another island. It seemed to be on fire.

As Nanna sailed closer, she saw the flames came from hundreds of camp fires. Some of the people sitting round them ran down to the beach to meet her.

"Tasty morning!" they shouted. "Tasty morning!"

Nanna was so surprised she didn't say anything.

"Haven't you got a tongue in your head?" shouted one man.

"Tasty morning!" said Nanna quickly. "Please, what are all those fires?"

"For cooking," said the man, and his companions smacked their lips. "Everyone's making new tastes."

"Can I try some?" asked Nanna, scrambling out of the boat, thinking of baked beans and tinned peaches.

"Try some smoked eel," said the cook at the first fire, "with seaweed relish."

"Quince-and-lemon sauce," the second cook said.

"Mousse of mulberry," said the third cook.

"I never knew there were such tastes," said Nanna.

"Everything tastes," said the third cook. "Smoke and stone, happiness, sadness . . . and what do little girls taste of?"

"I think I ought to be going now," said Nanna nervously. "Thank you for the tastes."

Nanna turned and ran along the beach. Her egg-
stone was safe in her boat and at the top of the mast
the boat's blue tongue was fluttering.

"I'll go where you go," said Nanna.

And away she sailed over the salt swings and the
green slide of the sea.

After a while, Nanna sailed into a bright mist. Then a third island loomed up right in front of her; and there, under a rainbow tree, she found a beautiful woman with long red hair sitting at a loom.

"Tasty morning!" said Nanna politely.

"Whatever do you mean?" said the woman.

"I mean, misty morning!" said Nanna.

"Every morning's misty," said the woman. "I weave mist. You see these threads? Every warp is a scent. Every weft is a stink. I'm weaving a web of whiffs and aromas and perfumes and pongs."

"Where do they come from?" asked Nanna.

"Babies flowers food chimneys sewers books stones . . ."

"Stones don't smell," said Nanna.

"They certainly do," said the woman.

Nanna pressed her blue stone to her nose.

"You see?" said the woman. "Stone smells of rain. Everything smells. Books stones Paris rats kindness anger . . . they're all in my web."

"I think I can smell them," said Nanna. And she dawdled back to her boat, sniffing and smelling as she went. "Wherever I go," she said, "my nose goes first."

By the time Nanna reached land for the fourth time, it was already dark. As she stepped out of her little boat, fingertips frisked across her face.

"Who's that?" said Nanna, stepping sideways.

Then something like a nose rubbed against her right ankle.

"And that?" said Nanna.

All sorts of fingers and paws—firm and tender, smooth, rough, cold and slimy—began to pat Nanna's face and arms and stroke her hair. Then some of the fingers and paws started to pinch Nanna and scratch her.

"Gerroff!" yelled Nanna, diving back into the safety of the boat.

Nanna's skin was tingling. "Touch and go!" she exclaimed. With one hand she grasped the rough wooden tiller and, carefully putting the blue stone into her pocket, she trailed her other hand in the satin water.

"They were all touch, nothing but touch," said Nanna.

She lifted her hand from the cool water and, closing her eyes, began to explore everything within reach: the points of the anchor, the supple plastic bailer, the softness of eyelids and the hairiness of hair, the rough-and-smoothness of her riding over the bustling waves.

Just before dawn, Nanna sighted land again, a dark lump, a sleeping lobe. Then the darkness in the east wasted and somehow swelled grey and green; and there, standing on the beach, someone was waiting to meet her.

"Hello!" said the boy.

"It's you!" exclaimed Nanna.

"I said we'd meet again. I brought you here and I must take you home."

"How did you get here?" asked Nanna.

"Oh!" said the boy. "All these islands are mine. Listen to this!"

He ran a few yards along the beach, and under his tread the sand squeaked and creaked.

"Let me try!" said Nanna.

"Singing sands," said the boy. Then he picked up two large shells and put one to Nanna's ear.

Nanna entered a great cavern; she listened to all the far-off whispering and gossip of the sea.

"Now this!" said the boy. He raised the other shell to his lips and blew it. It bellowed. It roared and howled.

"Sea-music," said the boy.

"Let me try!" said Nanna.

Then the boy took Nanna by the hand and led her up from the beach into a little wood. All around them the air was shining and shimmering with birdsong.

"Oh! Oh!" cried Nanna. "Listen! It's as if I've never heard a single sound before."

"Can you hear what they're saying?" said the boy.

Nanna listened and listened. Words she heard, and half-meanings: "Lightoflightoflightoflight . . . Start! Start! . . . Overnightwater! Over! Over! Overnightwater . . ."

"Nanna!" whispered the boy.

"Wake up!" trilled the birds. "Wake up, Nanna! Wake up . . ."

Nanna opened her eyes. Her little room was singing with sunlight and her mother was standing at the end of her bed.

"Good morning, Nanna!" she said.

"Good morning!" said Nanna.

Nanna listened to the sunlight. She touched her tongue and tasted her journey. Nanna sniffed at something locked in her left hand. She looked up at her mother and smiled.